The Swamp
Where Gator Hides

By Marianne Berkes

Illustrated by Roberta Baird

Dawn Publications

To Glenn and Muffy, who make it possible for me to induce joy and wonder in my books. I love working with you all at Dawn Publications, as you continue to promote a greener, happier world! — MB

To my children, who are the inspiration and to Tyler who always knew. — RB

Many thanks to Interpretive Ranger Leon Howell of the Everglades National Park, and to Taylor Schoettle, author of A Naturalist's Guide to Okefenokee Swamp, for their generous assistance with the manuscript. Thanks also to The Hobe Sound Nature Center for use of the puppets.

Library of Congress Cataloging-in-Publication Data
Berkes, Marianne Collins.
  The swamp where Gator hides / by Marianne Berkes ; illustrated by Roberta Baird. -- First edition.
       pages cm
  Summary: Through rhyming text reminiscent of "The House that Jack Built," follows the activities of various animals and birds as they make their way through the swamp where Gator waits to catch his prey. Includes facts about swamps, particularly the Florida Everglades, and the animals that make their home there, as well as teaching tips.
  ISBN 978-1-58469-470-0 (hardback) -- ISBN 978-1-58469-471-7 (pbk.) [1. Stories in rhyme. 2. Swamp animals--Fiction. 3. Alligators--Fiction. 4. Swamps--Fiction. 5. Everglades (Fla.)--Fiction.] I. Baird, Roberta, 1963- illustrator. II. Title.
  PZ8.3.B4557Sw 2014
  [E]--dc23
                              2013026011

Book design and computer production by Patty Arnold, Menagerie Design & Publishing

The cover title font Trinigan FG was designed by Andreas Höfeld
Erbach, Germany — www.fontgrube.de

Manufactured by Regent Publishing Services, Hong Kong
Printed January, 2014, in ShenZhen, Guangdong, China

10 9 8 7 6 5 4 3 2 1
First Edition

DAWN PUBLICATIONS
12402 Bitney Springs Road
Nevada City, CA 95959
530-274-7775
nature@dawnpub.com

This is the algae
that carpets the swamp
where Gator hides.

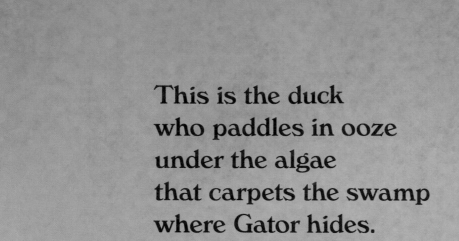

This is the duck
who paddles in ooze
under the algae
that carpets the swamp
where Gator hides.

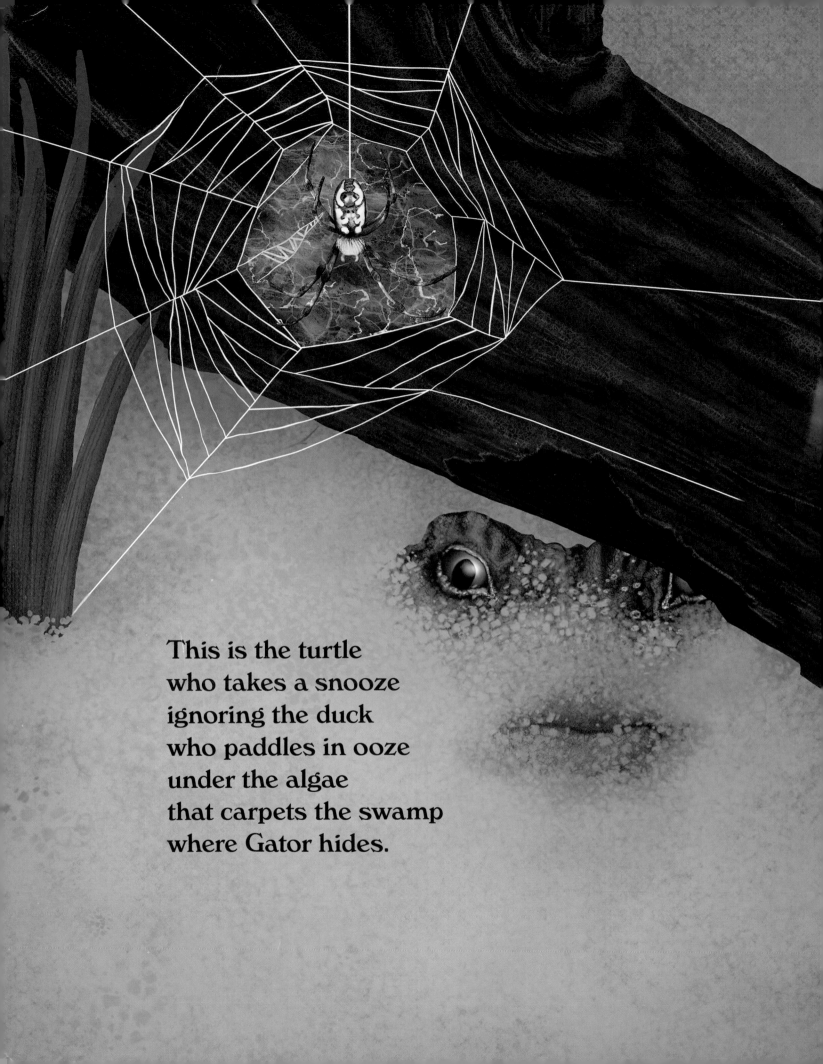

This is the turtle
who takes a snooze
ignoring the duck
who paddles in ooze
under the algae
that carpets the swamp
where Gator hides.

This is the snake
who slithers around
past the turtle
taking a snooze
ignoring the duck
who paddles in ooze
under the algae
that carpets the swamp
where Gator hides.

This is the frog
with a rumbling sound
eyeing the snake
who slithers around
past the turtle
taking a snooze
ignoring the duck
who paddles in ooze
under the algae
that carpets the swamp
where Gator hides.

This is the deer
who grazes nearby
the bullfrog with
a rumbling sound
eyeing the snake
who slithers around
past the turtle
taking a snooze
ignoring the duck
who paddles in ooze
under the algae
that carpets the swamp
where Gator hides.

This is the egret
nesting up high
who watches the deer
grazing nearby
the bullfrog with
a rumbling sound
eyeing the snake
who slithers around

past the turtle
taking a snooze
ignoring the duck
who paddles in ooze
under the algae
that carpets the swamp
where Gator hides.

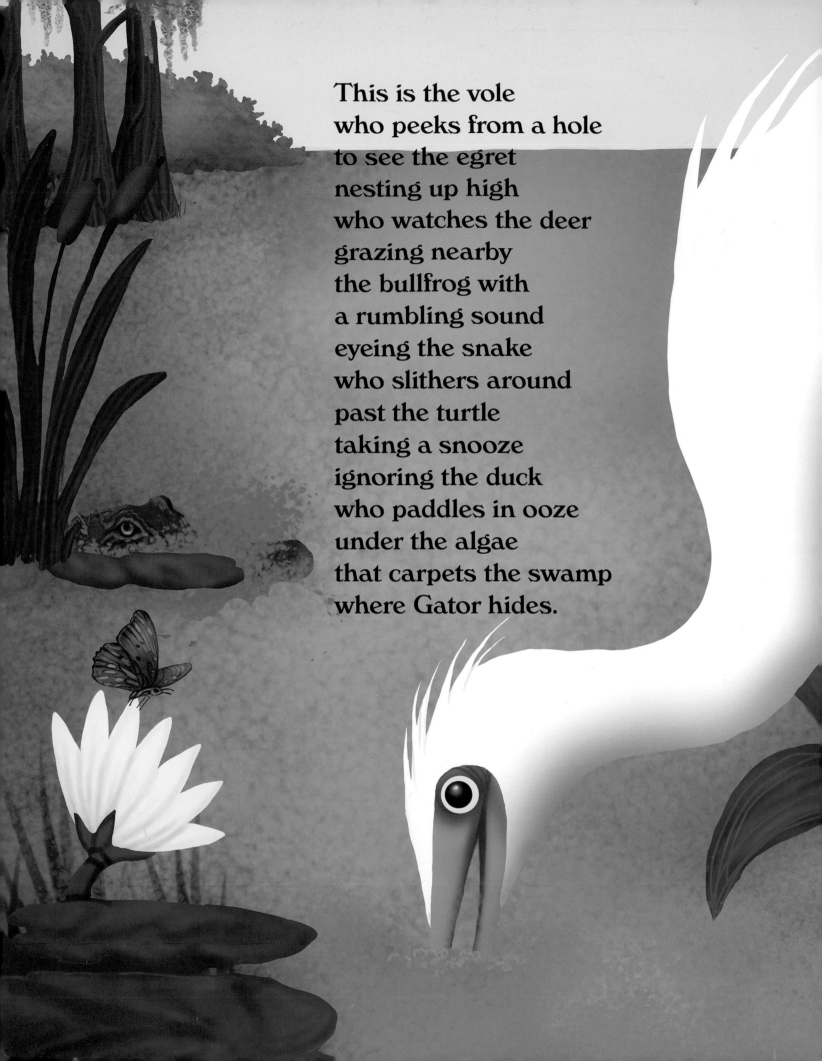

This is the vole
who peeks from a hole
to see the egret
nesting up high
who watches the deer
grazing nearby
the bullfrog with
a rumbling sound
eyeing the snake
who slithers around
past the turtle
taking a snooze
ignoring the duck
who paddles in ooze
under the algae
that carpets the swamp
where Gator hides.

This is the bobcat
taking a stroll
who stalks the vole
who peeks from a hole
to see the egret
nesting up high
who watches the deer
grazing nearby
the bullfrog with
a rumbling sound
eyeing the snake
who slithers around
past the turtle
taking a snooze
ignoring the duck
who paddles in ooze
under the algae
that carpets the swamp
where Gator hides.

This is the sunfish
who scoots away
when Gator comes out
to catch his prey.

WHO WILL HE HAVE FOR LUNCH TODAY?

Is it the bobcat
who took a stroll?

Or the vole
who peeked from a hole?

Is it the egret
nesting up high?

Or the deer
grazing nearby?

Is it the frog
with a rumbling sound?

Or the snake
who slithers around?

Is it the turtle
taking a snooze?

Or the duck
who paddles in ooze?

Under the algae
that carpets the swamp
where Gator NO LONGER hides.

A Swampy World

A SWAMP is a kind of half-land, half-water wetland habitat. Swamps typically have areas of shallow, slowly moving water among other areas of slightly more elevated, dryer land called *hammocks*. Swamps often occur near rivers and lakes. They are usually very fertile, having a mixture of decomposing plant matter, called *peat*, and soil. Water received as runoff from surrounding lands supplies many rich nutrients. Swamps can be in any climate from the Arctic to the Amazon.

Swamps are too wet for farmers to plant crops, so in the past, farmers typically drained swamps next to their fields to plant more crops. Today we know that swamps are critically important in providing fresh water and oxygen to all life. They act as purifying agents, improving water quality by filtering out nutrients and sediments from runoff. Conservationists and environmental agencies all over the world are now taking steps to protect and preserve swamps.

The swamp in this story is in the Florida Everglades, where a warm, wet, subtropical climate provides ideal conditions for alligators. Alligators are cold-blooded animals, meaning that they do not generate their own body heat as do warm-blooded animals. Across the southeastern United States, alligators like to sit in the warm, sometimes stagnant water of swamps beneath a blanket of floating leaves of water lilies, duckweed, and mats of floating algae. Aquatic algae are actually primitive plants which spread on the surface of the swamp. Alligators can hardly be seen under the floating cover except for their eyes. When prey comes too close, they lurch forward powerfully and suddenly to grab it, and . . . well, you never know what might happen next.

Gators and More

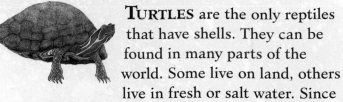

TURTLES are the only reptiles that have shells. They can be found in many parts of the world. Some live on land, others live in fresh or salt water. Since they are cold blooded, turtles can't live in places that are cold all year long. The Florida red bellied turtle in this story likes the warm wet swamp and spends a lot of time basking on a log in the sun. It is mostly vegetarian, but occasionally eats larvae, earthworms, and tadpoles.

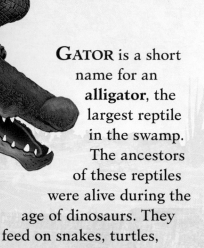

GATOR is a short name for an **alligator**, the largest reptile in the swamp. The ancestors of these reptiles were alive during the age of dinosaurs. They feed on snakes, turtles, fish, mammals, or just about anything. Alligators love the humid heat of subtropical swamps and dig huge holes in the mud. When drought occurs, these deep holes are the last things to dry up, providing an important source of water for alligators and other wildlife. Alligators are abundant in swamps from Texas to North Carolina. They are closely related to crocodiles. Crocodiles have more pointed snouts and their teeth can be seen even when their mouths are closed. Crocodiles also grow larger than alligators and are much more aggressive toward humans. Also crocodiles can tolerate saltwater while alligators prefer freshwater. South Florida is the only place where both alligators and crocodiles live.

DUCKS love to be around water. In swamps they eat grasses, aquatic plants, fish, insects, worms, amphibians and mollusks. The duck in this story, paddling in the still swamp water, is a "dabbling duck" that tips up its tail and puts its head underwater as deeply as it can to find food.

SNAKES that live in swamps are good swimmers. They often sun themselves at the water's edge and slither around looking for food. The snake illustrated in this story is the cottonmouth, also called a water moccasin. It eats fish, frogs, salamanders, small turtles, birds, small mammals, and even baby alligators. This large, poisonous snake is very dangerous! When bothered, it vibrates its tail and opens its mouth wide, revealing a white interior which is how it got the name "cottonmouth." It is sometimes confused with non-poisonous water snakes, so watch out!

BULLFROGS bask at the water's edge among the leaves of plants. The male bullfrog's deep rumbling croak sounds like "jug-o-rum" and can be heard over a distance of more than a mile. Some bullfrogs grow so large that they can capture and eat little birds and snakes, but mostly they eat insects and small fish. A frog's protruding eyes can see in several directions at the same time, even though they seem to stare blankly.

VOLES, sometimes called field mice or meadow mice, live in almost all of North America except very dry areas. They make nests using sedges and grasses from which they build underground burrows where they store food and where females give birth to their young. Voles breed frequently and have five to as many as ten litters a year. Voles also use tunnels to get around, enabling them to stay hidden from birds of prey—and, of course, alligators.

WHITE-TAILED DEER are found throughout North America, wherever there are grasses or leaves to eat. "White tailed" refers to the underside of the deer's tail, which it raises when it senses danger. This deer is long-legged, fast-moving, and high-jumping—it can jump over eight foot fences! Its speed is its main defense, as it is prey for panthers, bobcats and—in the swamps—even alligators.

BOBCATS are very adaptable, living in swamps as well as deserts, mountains, woodlands, and plains throughout almost all of North America. They are active day and night, and sleep only two or three hours at a time. They usually hunt small mammals, like voles and squirrels, but can take on an animal as large as a deer. Their claws make them excellent tree climbers, often surprising birds or pouncing on prey from trees.

EGRETS are graceful herons with long white feathers that cascade down their backs during the breeding season. The word "egret" comes from the French word "aigrette" meaning "brush." In the 1800's both the great egret, shown in this story, and the snowy egret were hunted almost to extinction for their plumes for ladies' hats. They were protected when put on the endangered list, and have now recovered. Egret nests are a platform made of sticks high up in trees. Egrets hunt by standing motionless in a swamp or pond, waiting for fish or other prey to come by.

SUNFISH are named for their bright, sunny colors. There are many different kinds of sunfish, but the one in this story lives in swamps and small ponds, swimming in water that has lots of plant growth. Sunfish have a strong homing instinct and return to spawn in the same vicinity each year. Males are more colorful than females.

Tips from the Author

The Swamp Where Gator Hides is a variation on *The House That Jack Built* that teaches cumulative story structure, rhyming, and sequence of events. How is this book different? How is it the same? Explain to students that a cumulative rhyme repeats each part of a story from beginning to end.

Rhyming Ask students to listen for pairs of rhyming words: ooze/snooze, around/sound, etc.

Sequencing Students can put events in order using strips that are downloaded at www.dawnpub.com (click on "activities") and cut apart. Or make your own strips, e.g. "who paddles in ooze," "who takes a snooze," etc.

Puppet Show Puppets come in every form imaginable, as you see in the photo. Or children can make their own using things at hand, such as paper bags, paper cups and plates, socks, or sticks with small pictures portraying the different animals in the story. Kids can also make a stage with a swamp setting to use as you read the story. A reader's theater for older students helps develop fluency and enhance comprehension. See: http://www.readwritethink.org/lessons/lesson_view.asp?id=172

Snip-Snap Gator Draw an alligator or trace it onto a recycled file folder. Cut into three separate pieces the upper jaw, lower jaw with body, and tail. Kids color scales, a red tongue, and glue on a google eye. Stick brass paper fasteners through the tail and the upper jaw attaching them to the body. Or make a clothespin alligator that "snaps." See: www.busybeekidscrafts.com/Clothes-Pin-Alligator.html

Playing with Poetry A *haiku* is an old form of Japanese poetry, often about nature. It has three lines. The first line has five syllables, the second line has seven syllables, and the third line has five. Ask kids to write one. Here is an example:

> *Algae covers swamps*
> *With carpets of slimy scum*
> *Gators hide in it.*

Go on a Fact Hunt Ask students to choose an animal in the book and write two facts about animals that are **not** in the book, and where they got their information (from books, the internet, a television show, etc.)

Books and websites

Catfish Kate and the Sweet Swamp Band, Sarah Weeks (Atheneum, 2009)

Marsh Music, Marianne Berkes (Lerner, 2000)

Marsh Morning, Marianne Berkes (Lerner, 2003)

Marshes and Swamps, Gail Gibbons (Holiday House, 1999)

Swamp Song, Helen Ketteman (Two Lions, 2009)

Wetlands: Soggy Habitat, Laura Purdie Salas (Picture Window Books, 2007)

www.education.nationalgeographic.com/education/encyclopedia/swamp/

www.exploringnature.org/ — in the main index, go to Wetlands of the World

www.enchantedlearning.com/biomes/swamp/swamp.shtml has printouts of swamp animals.

Bookmarks and Activities Click on "activities" at www.dawnpub.com and look for more of Marianne's curriculum-connection activities and reproducible swamp animal bookmarks, along with reproducible sequence of events strips.

Tips from the Illustrator

The pictures in this book may look like they were painted with traditional tools using paintbrushes and canvas, but they were actually painted digitally—that is, with a computer. That makes me a "digital illustrator."

Before I draw anything, I begin by researching the animals and the environments in which they live. It's very important to learn all that I can about the animals so that I can paint them accurately, and it's fun too!

This is me at my desk. I look at the screen as I draw and paint. I like the room to be a little dark as I work

This is a sketch that has been scanned into the computer and is ready to be colored in Photoshop.

This is one of the bottom layers of the illustration. As you can see there are no animals added yet.

The duck is finished and ready to be added to the illustration.

Here is the finished illustration. Now it's ready to save and send to the publisher.

The first step actually begins with a pencil and paper. I create many drawings of the animals, and then I sketch out the full pages as I want them to look. I must be sure to remember to leave space for the text when designing the pages. Once the pencil drawings for each page are done, I place each one on a scanner that copies the sketches and sends them as digital images to my computer.

Next, I open my sketches in a program called Photoshop. This program is like opening a big new box of paints that never get lost, spilled, or used up. There are many colors and brushes to choose from.

In front of my computer screen is a special tablet and a stylus, which looks very much like a pencil. Actually the stylus is sort of like a pencil, a marker, and a paintbrush all rolled in one! I choose colors from a palette, choose the type of "brush" I want my stylus to be at the moment, and start "painting" on the tablet. The tablet itself stays blank, but what I am doing with the stylus on the tablet shows up on the computer screen. With these tools I'm able to add as many colors, styles, and textures as you can possibly imagine.

When painting digitally, one thing that's very different from traditional painting is that each illustration is created in layers. For example, the background is one layer, and the animals are painted separately in a layer that goes on "top" of the background. This allows me to move the parts of the painting around, even after they're completely colored in. Sometimes there are many layers, so I try to carefully label each one, or it can get confusing.

What happens when I make a mistake? Did I just put horns on the alligator? No problem! All I have to do is "undo" a few steps, or delete the whole layer, and continue on. That's a big advantage of being a digital illustrator. But what is my favorite advantage of all over regular paint-and-brush illustrating? There's no paintbrush to wash or mess to clean up!

I love my job as a digital illustrator. It makes me very happy to learn, draw, and paint animals and all kinds of nature. I hope you've enjoyed learning about the animals in this book as much as I've enjoyed illustrating them.

Marianne Berkes has spent much of her life as a teacher, children's theater director and children's librarian. She knows how much children enjoy "interactive" stories and is the author of many entertaining and educational picture books that make a child's learning relevant. Reading, music and theater have been a constant in Marianne's life. Her books are also inspired by her love of nature. She hopes to open kids' eyes to the magic found in our natural world. Marianne now writes full time. She also visits schools and presents at conferences. She is an energetic presenter who believes that "hands on" learning is fun. Her website is www.MarianneBerkes.com.

Roberta Baird grew up loving both books and art. As an illustrator, she combines both of these passions to create whimsical pictures for children. Her house is full of pets, including Bailey (pictured), who is one of three dogs that, Roberta says, "own" her. There's also a cat, rats, a hermit crab, fish, and birds—including one very colorful Amazon parrot. Outside, right by her backyard in Texas, there is a swamp with turtles, bullfrogs, snakes and even a gator or two! Illustrating animals is one of her favorite things to do.

ALSO BY MARIANNE BERKES

Going Around the Sun: Some Planetary Fun — Earth is part of a fascinating "family" of planets. Here's a glimpse of the "neighborhood."

Going Home: The Mystery of Animal Migration — Many animals migrate "home," often over great distances. A solid introduction to the phenomenon of migration.

Over in the Arctic: Where the Cold Winds Blow — This charming rhyme introduces baby animals of the tundra while kids sing along and learn to count.

Over in Australia: Amazing Animals Down Under — Australian animals are often unique, many with pouches for the babies. Such fun!

Over in the Forest: Come and Take a Peek — Follow the tracks of forest animals, but watch out for the skunk!

Over in the Jungle: A Rainforest Rhyme — As with "Ocean," this book captures a rainforest teeming with remarkable animals. **Also available as an interactive app!**

Over in the Ocean: In a Coral Reef — With unique and outstanding style, this book portrays a vivid community of marine creatures. **Also available as an interactive app!**

Over in a River: Flowing Out to the Sea — Kids learn their geography — ten major rivers of North America — as well as counting the animals and babies that live in or around the rivers.

Seashells by the Seashore — Kids discover, identify, and count twelve beautiful shells to give Grandma for her birthday.

What's in the Garden?—Healthy fruits and vegetables are much more interesting when children know where they come from. And a few tasty recipes can start a lifetime of good eating.

New from Dawn — This book is available as an interactive book app! Look for gator hiding in the algae, then animate the turtle, vole, bobcat, duck, sunfish, and other animals that might be his lunch.

Dawn Publications is dedicated to inspiring in children a deeper understanding and appreciation for all life on Earth. You can browse through our titles, download resources for teachers, and order at **www.dawnpub.com** or call 800-545-7475.

1